ALL THIS COULD BE YOURS

ALL THIS COULD BE YOURS

poems

Joshua Trotter

BIBLIOASIS

FIRST EDITION

Library and Archives Canada Cataloguing in Publication

Trotter, Joshua
    All this could be yours / Joshua Trotter.

Poems.
ISBN 978-1-897231-96-8

    I. Title.

PS8639.R657A77 2010   C811'.6   C2010-904594-7

Edited by Zachariah Wells

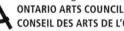

Canada Council   Conseil des Arts
for the Arts   du Canada

Canadian   Patrimoine
Heritage   canadien

ONTARIO ARTS COUNCIL
CONSEIL DES ARTS DE L'ONTARIO

Biblioasis acknowledges the ongoing financial support of the Government
of Canada through The Canada Council for the Arts, Canadian Heritage,
the Book Publishing Industry Development Program (BPIDP); and the
Government of Ontario through the Ontario Arts Council.

PRINTED AND BOUND IN CANADA

For a newcomer escaped from shipwreck and spending some time here in the course of his unknown destiny, these solitudes sometimes bring on a profound despondency: there is despair in the air. And then suddenly he feels a caress, a passing breath of air that raises his spirits. What is this breath of air? A note, a word, a sigh, nothing. This nothing is enough.

—Victor Hugo, *The Toilers of The Sea*

Contents

ALL THIS COULD BE YOURS

THEME OF THE PERPETUAL ARCHITECT

So I'm back at the corner drafting board
over which I am landlord and surveyor.
Here I prepare my latest, final lair
which I'll build by hand with cash and glass
and when the light is right I'll rest fulfilled
in my preferred Bauhaus chair, while snow
thrashes the windows like friends I once knew.

Oh Buckminster, Oh Frank Lloyd, you were right.
The frailest palladium is peace of mind.
A trailer-park is an isthmus of light.
Cohabitation is the shortest line
away from sane. Geodesic. Carmine.
To be alone this winter, I stay home
driving black lines through the white.

ALL THIS COULD BE YOURS

I know warm milk is not your cup of tea
so I've laid out a range of humble pies,
diet Cokes and angel cake, one small piece,
on prayer mats beneath the mistletoe
with modesty enough to make you pause,
rewind and press play for another pass
across the tableau prepared for your stay.

Notice the honest arrangement of grapes.
The platters from which flowers droop. Tired hands
of hired hands rendering the leafy ends
of emerald necklaces. Notice our grips
slipping, our gaunt expressions, how we stand
horse-legged, gasping, intemperate winds
blown thinking from the ledge, through the gap

between the frame and what it haunts for us.
I'd like to thank you for the extra mile,
the undead weight you muled like sacks of mail.
Almost everything grows here, and we use
hardly anything. Take this as a formal
request; Please join our team; The final meal
you'll walk towards in someone else's shoes.

TURING WORLD

I want a program to use a program which can simulate
a Turing's machine like Turing world. Where can I find it,
in light and free version!!! Thanks. —Anonymous

Decode the cries of birds, is why I came
at dawn to press record on each machine.
Oscilloscopes and spectrographs and hoists
grew hot then moist then rust I stayed so long
unknown among my future-perfect hosts.
I stayed so long and never heard them sing
a theme I couldn't transfer note for note
to satellites that thronged above unsung
repeating birdcall bleep for bleep—but not,
I told myself—restating what they sang.
I'd caught the pitch, the point remained unclear.
Dead air, I said, as I prepared to leave
for they, like me, had little to declare
so I declared and made myself believe.

LANDSCAPE WITH INTERFACE

It's hard to tell who's talking through the rain

to stop talking. Rather, stranger, listen:
The rain and your talking walk glove in glove

joggling together appeasable thumbs.

It's hard to tell if the rain is aping
a greater ape than you, stranger, speaking

in the first-person with apposite fluency.

What separates you from the mingling leaves,
from the quality or deficiency

of mood-lightning? Listen, It's hard to tell

who's speaking: Is this rain, or is this you
stranger, straining the scene with the pitter-

pattering patois of unopposable tongues?

ODE TO ESPERANTO

Yesterday someone told me that 'to wait'
and 'to hope' in Spanish share the same verb.
Now, I don't know about the Spanish, but
I do know the way a cat will drag a bird
or fresh mole to fester in the corner
till someone finds, or worse, steps in it
and bears it, shrouded in tissue paper
to a hasty ceremony above a toilet
and I do know, in English, that an ode
is not what's owed, rather, an elegy
for the meek and merely departed—Oh
ravaged mole, fondled bird, you flurries
of feathers and dirt, you dug and you flew
and lent these words small weights to cling to.

THE SOLOIST

She found relief on the dying reef in the middle of our bay.
I sent a team to see if she might need a pick-me-up
and heard singing, like last night's and the nights before.

Was she lost? Sent? Where she went when the tide came
we never knew. She dispersed by day, but by night
her voice from every plane, from every gleaming glass and plate.

Weeks proceeded. Pools grew. Singing soaked us through.
Our great house began to slouch. The time for action was on us.
We sent team two, in an expensive custom-built craft.

The tide was out. They rowed into it, lifting and dipping in unison
while singing beaded their brims. In the stern, below the boards
her singing rose. Records show they never made it home.

I've put in pipes and pumps, drains and troughs.
Agog behind me, my servants mop the walls with cloths.
My closest advisors lance glances at me—They hear her, I'm sure,

for it's not with sweat their clothes are wet, nor rain.
Her song slides down the sides of their bowed brains.
I listen to the drips, the drops and trickles. My kingdom drowns.

ABOUT FAITH *fig. 1*

Impalpable rodents
swarm
in shifting packs

change course
back
and forth and back

bounding over tines of grass
bending back tips
of grasses as they pass

marking paths
for the blind
wind behind them.

R.A.T.S.

The piper played forests.
We dashed with the rabbits.

The piper played deserts.
We flecked the white sand.

The piper played the moon.
We teed-off up there.

The piper played the sea.
We breathed choral air.

The piper play-by-played
and we topped the charts.

The piper played low.

We leaned close.

The piper hummed.

Closer we crammed.

The piper sat pie-eyed
and we went nowhere fast.

The piper held his breath
then cried, alone at last.

EXTERIOR. PÈRE JOSEPH'S CABIN. DAY.

This morning, Père Joseph is peering through the window of his narrow shack, somewhere northwest of the Sault, at the edge of a wide clearing, 1623. This is the first morning of the first winter of his first glimpse of sightlessness. On his back, Père Joseph carried these four panes, and all through summer's montage he sawed and planed and notched logs to lumber. He split, lifted, and fit in such a manner that time became a fixed system of angles and distances. His hopes became home. This morning the Père is neither elated nor afraid. Eyeing the window of his narrow shack, Père Joseph steps in to one middle of miles of distance. He touches the back of each of his teeth with his tongue.

PÈRE JOSEPH:
There is no middle distance.

Which is his first complete thought, or speech, in weeks. At the leaded glass, the growing blaze of snow on his face, Père Joseph is a statue carved from surprise. The expanse of sky and snow around him a blinding, widening maw. Père Joseph at the window of his narrow shack is the only syllable for miles.

PROPHETS AND LOSSES

This just in: Fatal plunge leaves bystanders
strangely illuminated. Blind-sided biker
glimpses stars. Woman reports purse-snatching
and visions of angels. A store-owner
recently robbed calls it "lightening the load."
Down the road, a burst of light, then sirens.

The wind is a whitewashed fence. The rimed sky
sea-grass wild with salt. We climb the rails
into light so deep we lose our sandals
like trilliums in late snow, we lose crested rollers,
lose frosted crullers, lose seasons, stars
from one-star beach-front resorts, lose reason.

After the parade there's nothing left
but loss itself. It's not about what comes
next, rather, what's the nexus?
We meet the surf, surf reaches out to us.
We preach love, our love besieges us.
We eat pale grapes and the seeds float like Jesus

whose hotwaxed Lexus keeps the saltwater out
for an instant, who goes under waving
and blinking, a sequined home-coming queen
who spots her parents in a sea of starry faces
and, blowing Morse-code kisses between each finger,
steps from her floating world to say hello.

THE TEACHER AND THE PEACH

"If you weren't bursting," her teacher informed her,
"you wouldn't need patience." —Philip Roth

The sky holds thunder as a swimmer
gone under holds air, holds the fist
of panic inside the chest like the first
flush of rapture reined-in, the way grammar
exploits the onrush of language,
the way skin grasps flesh about to burst,
the way lust is engine, all piston and breast
as a dam yokes the river's surge—
What drives you here? What drags you back
to displace again? What, if you catch it,
pulls you face-forward? What lull, what lack?
Wait, he says, don't say it. Save it.
I won't touch it. Don't need to know.
Be full fruit. Fall ripe. And never let go.

THEME OF THE DEEP SEA COOK

With no strings attached, I will soar
from my galley, wrenching lines
like deckhands in the storm of the year

handling the ends of my danglings
like real chef's knives
or the singular wigglings of a puppeteer.

They say a falling blade has no handle
they say ladle ladle ladle
they say no money down pay-up later.

With clenched fists and high interest I haul
these shrouds to see not who fails
but who climbs—

Ascending, they tell me, take the helm
of your abandon, get a handle
on yourself. Wait, don't leave me yet, says I.

THE INTERIOR OF AN EDIFICE UNDER THE SEA

The Wall of Whippoorwills in the Evening.
The Atrium of Fragrant Lilacs.
Gallery of Afternoon Naps, Curtains Fluttering.
The Balcony of Talc. Terrace of Lace.
Reflective Pools of Bathwater Cooling.
Sixteen recordings of Rainy Street-Hisses.
The Darkened Dome of Headlights Arcing.
The Holy Hall of Garbled Arguments.
The Hall of Wonderstorms. Hall of Frightening.
Three whole floors of Separate Sleeping Arrangements.
Parents Not Talking. Tractor Trailers Braking.
The Walkway of Dinnerware in Pieces.

LAMENT FOR THE LOSS OF LOSS

We know now coincidence has a law
that's lonelier than well enough
when well enough is left alone.

Counting knits before purls, at one
with nothing doing, no go, no dice,
our eyewitness, too, is too far gone.

No, nothing can't ever be wrong.
Stain the sheets of time and space,
the loss for words is nothing less.

The new loss fits much like old loss
only flashier, *chic*, proficient
with gadgets, comes again on call.

Our old loss rarely called at all
and when Boss died we never heard
the half of it. Left few remarks

besides a darkness on the dark.
Little gods came of that, no less
than a startled Stoic's stifled *hurrah*.

AN ACHIEVEMENT, BUT NOT THE END
OF THE STORY

The opening night you've aimed for always:
The rain is climbing the aquarium windows
of the studio washed white for your solo show.
You're calling it "*The things I fed the waves.*"
With crackers. *Je ne sais quois.* Chardonnays
and two tingling parents aglow from their halos
to their big toes, so proud of their omphalos
at the Stilton center of the storm, asway.

What kind of cheese is this, your uncle barks,
poking the Camembert, eyeing the art.
He can tell it's expensive by the fumes.
He knows your game, it's all in the frame.
The tricky part is when to stop, or start
smiling, and recognising, and going dark.

LEITMOTIV

Tonight we watched a halfway-decent movie
concerning loss of memory and/or love
driving our sheathed nerve endings to approve
an ending we didn't quite loathe or believe.
There was a gait to the movie, a groove
that slit our wits by shortwave,
slotting our thoughts through its intricate sieve.
We were enthralled and galled, at one remove.

Between barren groves of firm resolve
and a liberal vale of stoic reserve,
we'd been moved. We met at the stove
for cheese-toast and tea. All critiques saved
by the window's moon-blaze: It was grand, grave,
and granted our silence something substantive.

WIND MACHINE 2.0

In the truck with the men wending home,
the machine of the wind is rewound

and repacked in its styrofoam carton.
What remains of the wind is wind's sound.

There are times in the wind we're cartoon
crows, barrel-rolling across the screen

to the Front, to peck peck our remains:
A Verdun of the mind gone offline.

We were wounded here once, and again
we receive a small fortune per tonne

of the sound of the wind we return.
Here, the clowning around of the wind

is debriefed and reprogrammed. Rearmed
countless times over time's refined plan.

SHIFTWORK

Obscurely, yet most surely called to praise
the swaths and swathes of late September wind,
in what tributary might the warship
of my worship heave-to and pay tribute?
This wind, it cuts, it binds so many ways,
in what bay shall I make my stand? What lee?
And what will I say, out of the row
on the prow, to make myself heard?

This is the season of things gone awry,
this is the high treason of birds: They fly.
This is the sea-run in which we take turns
in the wheelhouse, crank-calling the engineer.
This is the reason we swab in our sleep
as geese, sobbing, sweep the ceiling of day.

THE QUEEN'S SILVER JUBILEE FLEET REVIEW

It's easy to forget a price
was paid to learn the world
is round. And wet. And warm inside.
With luck we'll learn again.
Our pride and joy say there's no rush
to rise to the occasion
while a rigid Admiral, scrubbed and flushed,
reviews the lit parade
with hopes to score another glimpse

below the decks, a flash
of skin between the bows,
a disembodied peep, to throw
the sheets off everything:
That night beside the fire, his niece,
spinning, shows him things.
He learns again the hollow
ringing Earth is hallowed,
the ring around the globe is flesh.

Full-ahead, thirty man-o-wars
lay bare Her navy's oeuvre.
Their elegant manoeuvres
divert our prying eyes
to skirt around the centerpiece
of flame, the vast surprise
disguised within the spray and wash
the skirt around the burning bush
protects the bush from fire.

PRAYING WITH MATCHES

The last match won't make up its mind.
A match made not in heaven but some ethereal glade.

Like the scrub and stubble
behind Car Quest Auto Parts' reputable façade.

A seasonless service centre, a glowing saloon
of seized machines where one man's tire iron

is another's leaning mizzen, where there's no wreckage
to rectify, no knots to tie, no notion of the roiling, perilous ocean

to cling to. Behind Car Quest Auto Parts
we're building a sail-barge of cigarettes and cardboard

waiting for the tide to lift and the wind to shift
from the lapsed wrack of some future

where we suture this match, our last, unlit
to the prow; Our rugged bowsprit.

ABOUT FAITH *fig. 2*

Tonight you place your canoe
in care of the dark;
The dark holds

the canoe
and you
on a solid shelf of itself.

CONFESSIONAL

If dead ringers grin, my image wears one.
Gawking at myself for years, I know
what goes around comes back with parity.

The mirror is the pilot of the parody
whose job is to negotiate the torrent
between decoy and real McCoy.

The mirror is a pirate of veracity
on whose shoulder showboaters come to blows,
the centerpiece of the lab museum.

Beyond the exhibit, the weather's habit
grows disheveled. Wind transmits leaves
up-to and around, praising my edifice.

Devoted rain embraces, but does not at all
penetrate these scientific fortifications.
In his stall, at the axis of the squall,

Alex, the African Grey, calls to his likeness,
*Be not afraid my brother, I believe
the Centre will hold—*

We know today that parrots freely reason
across permanent pigeonholes, thanks
to anxious, habitual investigators

at the borderline Centre of Attention.
What's outside doesn't enter into it.
Examining the o-rings of original sin,

encountering cyclone season offshore,
Drs. *Blank* and *Blank* in padded think tanks
repeat, *tink tink*, this rosary ad nauseum.

PROPORTIONAL REPRESENTATION

Drawing away from all of our meetings
we contrived to pull meaning from trees.

The sky darkened. Some birds chirped. Nothing else.
It's not easy to leave all this behind.

The ride was long and uncomfortable.
We watched russet hills change shades in the rain.

The profile of every tree as we passed
was vast with simile, without 'like' or 'as.'

When we stopped for Cokes at a roadside stand
the guy there said he'd seen nothing like it.

An Airstream trailer agleam in the blush,
fallow orchards lolling with fruit.

Wow, we're so formless, pushing forty,
falling away from all our old seams.

Replacing meaning ain't easy, he said,
but it sure as hell beats raking these leaves.

CONTINUATION OF THE HISTORY OF UTOPIA

There were 'birds' whose purpose was to record
the movements of the masses, to repeat
working-class conversation verbatim.
I remember duplicate silhouettes
along power lines, where they'd match up
and watch us talk hand-in-hand in the dusk.
Their eyes were peepholes we couldn't shrink from;
Pinpricks the crimson sunset seeped through.
And yet, in less time than predicted, we'd quit
describing the incised rubies of their eyes
or questioning to whom they sang their reports.
We lived as always, sporting and shopping
and pausing at times to noiselessly cheer
some crow, confused by the cameras,
gouging lenses loose, enraged by their beauty.

THEME OF THE INVESTIGATIVE GENERALIST

Once the halved-lady pulled herself together,
once the sea lions left, clapping flippers,
once the tightrope seraphs had fallen
fast asleep, I was blinkered all alone
to think upon the crassness of my acts
of burning contradiction: The fuse was lit
blasting me through the roof-flap like a rocket.

Gasping sensibly due to lack of facts,
I look back: There's a gap, a blacked-out O
in the snowed-over parking lot where once
after nine sober months of sinking sales
Earth's Greatest Peepshow circled her trailers
to gather replacements, momentum, and practice
this new act, The Man Adrift In Vacuo.

EXTERIOR. PÈRE JOSEPH'S CABIN.
DAY FOR NIGHT.

He lived there in the unsayable lights.
The bread for his toast home-baked, oats
imported by mule from Sault St. Marie.
What he returned to the locals, who knew?
He ministered weekly to the weak few
who could make it. His mule acquired two
gangrenous protrusions. *If there were a way
out of here*, thought the Père after toast
with black tea, *would I take it?* New snow flew
landed and grew. Père Joseph stranded
in the familiar lattice he knew
would easily end him; So tight, the strands
were strings, hauling jowls of wolves to vowels
prowling the void above his drifted house.

WINTER IN THE KINGDOM OF WINDOWS

Skies release seas, and seas, by proxy, grant landfalls.
Spelunkers are sub-captains and fishermen sawyers.
Taxidermists are pilots rending and mending and rending

and mending the river's skin. An icebreaker is a painter,
psychologists skydive, meridian means just passing through.
'Another lonely window' is an oft-repeated peasant ballad;

The unpleasant tale of Father Joe's lonely window journey.
To us, a Joe-job is no joke. A Joe-job entails losing
and gaining and losing hope. Rope is our verb "to bear."

We say, "The ice-breaker's brush ropes down
on blank, frameless canvas." Or, "We last saw Father Joe
weeks ago, on snowshoes, roping North-North-East."

'Another lonely winter' is the hymn we unspool at funerals
loud and dear through the open eyelets of the dead,
intoning the thread Father Joe will someday follow home.

TAILORS OF THE SEA

Windows of paint-splotches. Wasps squashed-flat.

Windows of cobwebs, rigging, cotton, clot.

Windows of likely rain. Windows not facts.

Windows of mild applause. It moves us not.

Windows on eggshells. Windows of locked

opportunity, winnowing the stones we throw.

Shattered windows wintering as weathered flocks

at off-track betting windows, ground windows

drawn from the embittered Norse *vindauga*

stitching *vindr*, the wind, to *auga*, the eye

through the needling wind's *aye aye*, the sky

is fleeting / fluvial / a patchwork flotilla

of old Norse oarsmen sewing down the waves

encircling a planet / rowing pointlessly away.

ANOTHER LONELY WINTER

The back and forth and back of us
miles out, alone in all this white,
this lifeboat's built for more, my sweet

though all I know is you and me
I fear there's someone here with us
who bates each breath to match our oars.

•

Balloon of speech or tell-all sail,
each breath's blank option swells with fear
then tacks like hell around the point

of resolute indifference
whose tacit shoreline trimmed with fleece
lures anchorites and divorcees.

•

My sweet, put something on your feet,
the caption says we've sighted land
but through this haze it's hard to tell

whose voice is whose; That noise, my sweet
is tongues of waves or teething reefs
or shush now, whose fingers at whose lips?

HEARING

Mornings after we gave up words, we still loved
to lie and graze the day awake
watching our old chit-chat thatch the street like rain.

Blessed are the dead that the rain rains upon
now the dead grow sound limbs to stand upon
nourished by discourse we once loved.

In their sodden crypts they sigh awake
solitary, listening to the rain
heartened by our lost and rousing homilies—the rain

engaging vacant brains it falls upon
until everyone we love or once loved
is dying tonight or lying still awake

listening, for our sake, as rain rains the dead awake.
There's something diplomatic about rain
strewing phrase upon phrase upon...

But here I pray that none whom once I loved
hold words they love from rain. I'm held awake
by heavy sentences the rain might lay upon them.

JAILBIRDS

The hoard of hoots and chirps outgrew my archives
so I rationed the air in which they flew.

I hauled the wind through tubes. The rain, with gloves,
I hammered into lynchpins, flywheels, screws

and skewered the quivering thing to earth.
To thankless jerks it was a jungle gym.

To me, it was a triumph of great girth
worth every small *coup*, every calculation.

Is it luck then, or detailed engineering
that sparks the lack of interest in my work?

They cruise the park and park beyond the ring
of lights to curse and mock me through the dark

where hidden mikes squeeze every squeak and squawk—
taunts and all—to a file marked *Birds: In Song*.

THEME OF THE OUTCAST ORNITHOLOGIST

The hubbub often reaches us from the outermost fields,

the deep attention span of our innermost thinking.

Crows calling other crows are distant inklings

linking themselves. Catcalling crows

are subliminal sentries; *All's well*

All's well, along the great wall

dividing your minds

from mine.

PÈRE JOSEPH ON THE DIFFICULTY OF OPENING COMMUNICATIONS WITH THE NEUTRALS

In the absence
of the first person singular,
he/ she/ we sit

waiting for someone or some
other
to talk with.

Downstream from each rock
a small wave
stays in place

over which
smaller waves
wash.

This is the short story
of our English
they say, as waves

of words widen
vees of geese
from each mouth.

ABOUT FAITH *fig. 3*

We spoke and perceived reply.

Our shelters were audibly stocked.

In the kiss of fridge-lips we sounded.

Pickerel split meniscus.

PRESENT

What went before was no rehearsal.
A world comprised of four-fifths water
leaves little fodder for a dry run.
Our vessels—worked to work like fish
or birds, or suns—are time machines
and later, when we look them over,
away they look in cool refusal.

So sure I've wrought translucent flesh,
not otter's nests of reeds and needles,
my crowded, knotted, hot-wired freighters
are twisted drive-by tongue-reversals;
Looking back is my year-old father
leaning towards this leaning candle,
composing his first dying wish.

A wishing well makes no rebuttal.
The world impressed upon its mirror
is easily impressed by coins
and bricks and cast-off guns, the splash
of pure reward. Oblivion's
a flashy gift, just flip it over:
It barely looks like anything at all.

GEMINI

We don't want other worlds... We want mirrors.
                                    —Stanislaw Lem

My vacant looks and I stay home
scanning the sky for likenesses
while off they blast, steel picks in hand
through the fracture re-opened
in the motherlode behind my eyes,
the rupture I mime like a daughter
mining movement from the mirror
of her dear mama, in her own time.

They say we become our relations
and because they say so, we do.
The power of suggestion loads
our parents into our faces, though
they rarely say which we'll become
and so we're twins, falling home
two by two, the friction so great
we burn our plans to live alone.

Mirror, mirror, what is the variance
between these spreading veins I follow
in my cracked, antique vanity
and the vane-guided engines
that carbon date the sky with lines?
What wrinkled clouds and shifting faces
have launched uncounted prospectors
to join your dotted chromosomes?

THE PORPOISE

Among my Lucky Charms I find the prize.
It doesn't look as slick as on the box,
the flippant plastic lacks hydrodynamics.
When I stick the device beneath my gown
the moving parts aren't moving for my sake
so I smooth the lines, rub them sleek
lacking nothing but reason or purpose.

My purpose leaps and does backflips and grins
at me, or seems to frown, it's hard to tell.
I've got the badge for saving lives, but still
it takes more skill than mine to swim with poise.
My daily goals and I are training.
The heated water park is steaming.
Tonight I set the wave machine to Drown.

AS THE ADMIRAL HIMSELF WOULD HAVE BEEN THE FIRST TO ACKNOWLEDGE

Used sparingly, death may be a lifesaver.
Though weightless, insubstantial, ordinary
mortality adds and subtracts, reminding
the living there's a constant wavering here.
Those stars, for instance, look a little fey
without the black backdrop, and without sinking,
the sea's all sun and games. A lack of air

exhilarates me more than breathing easy;
I promise not to hold you up with nothing
less than the sum of all my parts, the weather
shows great potential, there's a mantic ray
of hope across the surf, the moon is rising
hey, survivors, keep those faces underwater;
Don't watch too close, best let it float away.

PSALM OF THE HAND

I was much further out than you thought
And not waving but drowning. —Stevie Smith

Blessed is the woolgatherer waving
at the distant white eiderdown of shore
while, blindsided by summer, we pose
towheaded among hops-emboldened brothers
leaning against the towering guard's chair;
Our dreams, day and night, plagued by teams
of babes in season, whose bleating leapings
are not squandered, whose fleece prospers.

Not so cocky! There are flocks of clouds
the wind tows away, parched sandcastles
will not stand judgment day, nor parasols
outlast throngs of drunken roughhousers.
The sun bronzes lifeguards and tough guys
but the hand of the waverer will flourish.

MORE SUSPICIOUS FACTS

I wish to die a eulogist
whose quietus will leave bereft
a world with all the benefits
of doubting Thomas Edison.
Inventor, father, figurine,
a filament for passing thoughts,
he set the dingy night adrift
on light, and jettisoned the rest.

By two-way telegraph he rings:
*Great news! Shocked scientists say no
nothing exists! There's no nothing!*

And so I charge my eulogy
with all the nothing never here.
A world devoid of darkness, there's
a rubber dinghy set afloat
on what? Warm air? Without doubt
to buoy my certainties, I'm heir
to everything: The atmosphere
stress-free, sans electricity.

THE LION'S SHORE

Drawn to the square like rollers up a coast,
lions sniff what chattels might be theirs
then back out how they came, reverse-camber,
slow dissolve of these unsociable climbers
whose reeled-in depth-of-field gets snared
on one last thorny problem of the forest:

A cornered spider, one of many eyes,
unblinking, panning past the washed-up man
telling truths as best he can to the camera
while reviewers catalog last errata
on ticket stubs, appraising *mise en scène,*
pacing, sub-sub-plots too trying to summarize

except by judicious jump-cuts and lying
around, impulsive dips in the fountain
holding hands wandering the piazza
thanking lucky stars for this *tabula rasa*
so blank the lions fear some frank deception
that they can't claw through, or even die trying.

WELCOMING PARTY

Is this what I've been traveling toward
dodging rocks and reefs at funereal speed?
I see no dish of milk, no welcoming lips
just this beach—palms outstretched—and the abyss
of all I've missed, winking from every bead
on every rain-whetted, wind-brandished blade.

SUPER CENTRE

They carry pitchforks, hockey sticks and burning brands.
They nurse snotty, jaundiced babies, birds in cages,
infectious diseases—and here's another thing:
I too clutch consequences of a kind.
Across the shattered parking lot they wait
and watch me try to look like I've got something
special on my mind. But really, it's just clots
of thought, like where to turn and how to stand
and how, beyond a blackened Mega Store, another crowd
stands gauzy in the asphalt-heated air. They're watching
further figures up the highway I can't see.
There are no cars or minivans. No aircraft making tracks
across the firmament. We've outdistanced old
ungainly metaphors. We're out to make some sense
of signs or gestures. When we do, we walk, not talking,
join another crowd. It's tiring. It rains. And crows
call further crows that only crows can hear.
Often, I'm weighted by this notion: Crows relay
amazing information all across the planet's surface-
tension. Mostly, I've got this burden of my own to bear.

GIANT SAVINGS

Real monsters buy stocks
in makers of cheap seeds
who sell to any Jacques
with a nicked axe to grind,
a weather eye for scores,
old Germanic fixer-uppers
with encephalic headroom,
walled gardens gone wild,
seedpods brash as bull-
steaks lashed to rice-stalks
rising from ashes and oaks
through fair-trade winds
ascending through flocks
of fuming gnats, chanting
"Hell no, we won't grow"
into the gardens of giants
in the land of family values
and indescribable bargains.

DIAMOND IN THE ROUGH

Amid the endless miming desert slate
I come across what seems to be a marriage
of mines. As in, "What's mine is yours to dig"
or else, "Let not the mirage of two minds
obscure the light that trues each mirrored edge
with every mirrored edge." Germane collage
of grooms and brides in petticoats of white.

The grooms and brides in petticoats of white
assume, like loved-ones round a many-tiered
and unscathed wedding cake, the right to drill
their sweetest teeth into this Lotusland
of wealth, or else, with prospects almost nil
I stumble, lonely, on a single lily mired
amid the endless miming desert slate.

HOME AND DERANGE

A missing sister. A murdered herd.
Contusion. Confusion. Mistaken word.
A family plot bought-out by the railroad
and there's only one way to make it right:
I hate to say *black* or *white*, rather, *might*
makes right, in which familial landscapes
bathe and rebathe in conflicting cathode rays.
Trees turn black. Stars make maps. Windows warn us
and, resorting to flashbacks, windows warm us
as we pause in the pitch beyond a house
to bask in a shaft of domestic light:
A father bathes a child. The dog's asleep.
At the kitchen table, a fork, a knife,
a vacant seat. A lamp is lit. Sit. Eat.

CAPTAIN FROST AT MIDNIGHT

Finally, Son, when your dreaded inner power
reveals itself to be the Real Big Deal
leaping forth in a froth of frost or fire,
you must choose for yourself: Good or Evil.
Will your means be reprieves or reprisals?
Will you be robbing banks or busting robbers?
As if there's no frieze between upheaval
and peace, no thaw between law and ordure.

Truth is, The Truth are a tribe we've enslaved
to clear the air so we can take it easy
making great decisions in the mountains.
The Truth, my son, bulldozes my indifference.
The Truth erects a fortress in the valley
then dethrones me as I pace my cave above.

The air here circumscribes the apple trees
and I trace their sparkling spheres, then retire,
sliding back on my tracks, inverse striptease,
to slouch in cape-and-costume by the fire.
From here I watch your dramas and comedies
pitching and convulsing on the grate:
I must be careful not to let them melt me
or go running to help you—choose—it's late.

THE LAWS OF INNOCENCE

We place our trust in wide open spaces
and just as likely in windows locked fast.
In dust and sometimes robots.
In airbags, windlasses, D-cups.
We trust in ego-nulling vistas, twins,
baked goods, bad jokes, winsome failure
of nuclear reactors, belaboured loss
of innocents, truth's abstractions
and that's nothing. Lately our old truisms
have returned to streetcars and food courts
smirking from silk-screened ball-caps and tees.
Try us, they tease, Pace your trust with nothing.
Nothing will persevere. Nothing will last.
Nothing is nothing if not relentless.

The first and last lines of TURING WORLD are variants from Robert Frost's "And Never Again Would Bird's Song Be The Same." The epigraph comes from a list of potential Turing Test questions at: http://greatbird.com/turing/turings.php?yr=1999.

R.A.T.S. is an acronym for Relocatable Automated Targeting System. It also stands for Robot Anti-Terror Squad, an ill-fated toy line of the early 1980s.

LAMENT FOR THE LOSS OF LOSS contains reworkings from Karen Solie's "Action at a Distance" and Charles Wright's "Basic Dialogue." My apologies to both authors.

AN ACHIEVEMENT, BUT NOT THE END OF THE STORY takes its last line from Philip Larkin's "Essential Beauty."

The first and last lines of SHIFT WORK hail from Richard Wilbur's "Praise in Summer."

PROPORTIONAL REPRESENTATION is for Mid-System Jockeys and Compilation Technicians across the land. "The sky darkened. Some birds chirped. Nothing else" is plucked from Irving Layton's "A Tall Man Executes A Jig."

The first and last lines of EXTERIOR. PÈRE JOSEPH'S CABIN. DAY FOR NIGHT began their careers in Seamus Heaney's "Glanmore Sonnet VI."

HEARING makes use of the following four lines from "Rain," by Edward Thomas: "Blessed are the dead that the rain rains upon:/ But here I pray that none whom once I loved/ Is dying tonight or lying still awake/ Solitary, listening to the rain."

AS THE ADMIRAL HIMSELF WOULD BE THE FIRST TO AKNOWLEDGE takes its title from John Ashbery's "Memories of Imperialism."

HOME AND DERANGE is for Zach Gaviller.

The epigraph, and the titles for a number of poems in this book have been gleaned from James Hogarth's translation of Victor Hugo's *The Toilers of the Sea*.

Prenatal versions of some of these poems appeared in *Arc*, *Grain*, *Descant*, *The Boston Review*, *Jailbreaks: 99 Canadian Sonnets* (Biblioasis) and *This Grace* (littlefishcart press). Thanks to the editors and publishers. Thank you, too, to the Canada Council for the Arts and the Ontario Arts Council.

Big-time thank you to Evan and Kelly Green-Podd, Rebecca and Jason Dalfen-Brown, Mendy and Rosalie Dalfen, Shawn Adler, Laura Messer, Jay and Marcelina Hayes-Salazar, Jenny Gleeson, Fraser Smith, Caleb and Eli Robinson, John Climenhage, Mathias Kom, Amy Chartrand, Zach Gaviller, Daniel Renton, Linda Besner, Gordon Johnston, Bernadette McGuigan, Dan Wells and everyone at Biblioasis, Grace E. Winterpumpkin, David Fleming, Caitlyn Gaudet, my brother Dylan, and my parents David and Nancy.

Zach Wells, you are a rock and you rock.

John David Bryce Ondrovcik, thanks for being impatient.

Jeramy Dodds, Gabe Foreman and Leigh Kotsilidis, thank you thank you thank you. What can I say that you guys couldn't say better?

Aliya, thanks for being patient. This book is for you.